17

50p

GORDON THE GHOST
and
Sarah Jane

written by Linda Dearsley

illustrated by Margaret Chamberlain

Macdonald

Sarah Jane was the tidiest child in the world.
She was also the cleanest child in the world
and it was driving her parents mad.

They all lived in a smart new house
on a smart new estate, but even that
wasn't good enough for Sarah Jane.
She inspected the corners for hidden dirt,
she inspected the washing for stubborn stains
and every night before she had a bath,
she inspected the tub with a magnifying glass.

Her parents were in despair.
Sarah Jane's mother was an artist
and Sarah Jane was always cleaning up her paints
and tidying away her pictures
before she'd finished painting them.

Sarah Jane's father mended cars and Sarah Jane
wouldn't even let him in the house
until he'd taken off his greasy overalls
and washed his hands at the garden tap.

'Sarah Jane, why don't you come and do some
finger painting with me?' suggested her mother.

'Yuk! Not likely,' said Sarah Jane.
'I'd get my hands all dirty.'

'Sarah Jane, why don't you come and help me
mend a car?' suggested her father.

'Yuk! Not likely,' said Sarah Jane.
'I'd get oil all over my clothes.'

Then one day, Sarah Jane's mother found her
Hoovering the cat and she got quite cross.
'Sarah Jane go away! Go and sweep the grass
if you've nothing better to do.'

Sarah Jane had already got the broom
out of the cupboard before she realised that
her mother was being sarcastic.
'Oh well. I'll show them,' sniffed Sarah Jane.
'I'll go for a long walk
and they won't see me all day!'

Sarah Jane set off down the road.
She walked away from the new estate,
down the hill, past the school,
and on and on until she came to the empty house
at the bottom of the narrow lane.

But what Sarah Jane didn't know was that
the house wasn't empty anymore.
Gordon the ghost had moved in.

Gordon the ghost had been looking for a house
to haunt for simply ages.
When he drifted past the old dark house
at the bottom of the narrow lane,
he knew it was the perfect place.
The gate was falling off its hinges
and the garden was so overgrown,
you could hardly see the house.

'What a lovely spooky garden,' said Gordon,
floating over the weeds.
'Deadly Nightshade – my favourite.'
And when he saw the house,
he thought it was wonderful.
It only needed a few touches to make it
the perfect spooking spot.

Gordon the ghost got to work at once.
He knitted some cobwebs and trailed them
all over the banisters.

He sprinkled speckled dust
upstairs and down,

and he sprayed the whole house
with a very nasty smell.

When he'd finished, it was the creepiest,
spookiest house, a ghost could wish for.

Better still, he found a trunk of old clothes
in the attic and he spent hours dressing up
and pretending to be dozens of different ghosts.

There was only one problem.
Gordon had nobody to haunt.

He practised his sighs and moans
but there was no one to hear them.
He put on his costumes
but there was no one to see them.
'What's the use of a haunted house,
if nobody knows it's haunted?' wailed Gordon.

Then one day Gordon looked through his spyhole
in the boarded-up window, and saw Sarah Jane.

Sarah Jane walked through the gate
that was falling off its hinges
and stared at the garden that was so overgrown
you could hardly see the house.

'What a dreadful overgrown garden,'
said Sarah Jane stomping through the weeds.
'Deadly Nightshade. Yuk!'
And when she saw the house she thought it was awful.
'What a dirty awful house,
someone ought to clean it up.
Good thing I've got my feather duster.'

Gordon the ghost was chuckling with glee.
'At last! A visitor!' he cried.
And clutching his white sheet around him,
he floated downstairs wailing,
'Wooo wooo ooooh . . .' in his scariest voice.

The only trouble was, Sarah Jane wasn't scared.
She never watched television and she only read
educational books, so she'd never heard of ghosts.
'Oh dear,' she said looking up at Gordon,
'have you got a tummy ache?'
'Wooo wooo wooo,' said Gordon, 'hooo.'
'Yes you said that just now,' said Sarah Jane,
flicking away a cobweb.

Gordon the ghost went back to the attic.
'I'd better find something more frightening,'
he said and he put on his pirate costume.
'Wooo! Hooo wooo,' he moaned
but Sarah Jane still wasn't scared.
'Oh dear,' she said looking at his eye patch,
'have you hurt your eye?'

Well Gordon the ghost tried on all his costumes
but Sarah Jane wasn't frightened by any of them.
She just kept on dusting and wiping and
Gordon's house got cleaner and cleaner
until in the end Gordon began to cry.

'Oh dear, what *is* the matter?' asked Sarah Jane.

'You're ruining my house,' wailed Gordon the ghost.

'Ruining it? No I'm not, I'm just making it
a bit more comfortable for you.'

'Comfortable?' snuffled Gordon,
wiping his nose on his sleeve.

'Yes! Clean, tidy, fresh, neat, spick and span,'
said Sarah Jane, passing him her hanky.

'But those were my best cobwebs and my nicest dust.
Haunted houses have to have cobwebs,' said Gordon.

'Nobody will ever come here to be haunted
if you keep the place looking like a tip,'
said Sarah Jane firmly.

'And you'd better let me take those costumes
to the dry cleaners. You can't answer the door
looking like that!'

Gordon wandered backwards and forwards
through a wall, while he thought things over.
Perhaps she was right. Perhaps that was where
he was going wrong, but he knew he was right
about the cobwebs.

'O.K. then, we'll try it your way,' he said at last.
'And I'll help you with the cleaning,'
interrupted Sarah Jane.
'But there's one condition,' added Gordon
with a mysterious smile . . .

People don't know what to make of Sarah Jane these days. She doesn't tidy the house anymore and one day, she even asked her mother for some black paper and pot of white paint –

and for the first time in her life,
Sarah Jane had to get just a little bit dirty.

A MACDONALD BOOK

© in the text Linda Dearsley 1987
© in the illustrations Margaret Chamberlain 1987

First published in Great Britain in 1987
by Macdonald & Co (Publishers) Ltd
London & Sydney
A BPCC plc company

Printed and bound in Great Britain by
Purnell Book Production Limited
Member of BPCC Group

Macdonald & Co (Publishers) Ltd
Greater London House
Hampstead Road
London NW1 7QX

British Library Cataloguing in Publication Data

Dearsley, Linda
    Gordon the ghost and Sarah Jane.—
    (Picture book fiction)
    I. Title   II. Chamberlain, Margaret
    III. Series
    823'.914 [J] PZ7
    ISBN 0-356-11785-5
    ISBN 0-356-11786-3 Pbk